The Dog Looks Happy Upside Down

Also by Meg Pokrass

Damn Sure Right (Press 53, 2011)

Bird Envy (Harvard Bookstore, 2013)

*My Very End of the Universe: Five Novellas-in Flash
and a Study of the Form* (Rose Metal Press, 2014)

Cellulose Pajamas–Prose Poems (Blue Light Press, 2015)

Grateful acknowledgement is made to the following journals, in which many of these pieces first appeared in different forms:

Flash Fiction International Anthology, Green Mountains Review, PANK, The Literarian, Failbetter, storySouth, JUKED, Wigleaf, SmokeLong Quarterly, Necessary Fiction, New World Writing, Journal of Compressed Arts, FRIGG, The Dr. T. J. Eckleberg Review, Yalobusha Review, NANO Fiction, Fwriction Review, Two Serious Ladies, Camroc Press Review, Thumbnail, Heavy Feather Review, Salome, Poetic Diversity, Prime Number.

The following stories appeared in *Damn Sure Right* (Press 53, 2011). Reprinted with permission.

"Like A Family"
"Them"
"Pounds Across America"
"California Fruit"

"In This Light"
"Vegan"
"Needles"
"Foreign Accent Syndrome"

Additionally, creative changes were made to the following stories: "Plastic Pool," "Toxins," and "Goldswack."

The Dog Looks
Happy Upside Down

Meg Pokrass

Etruscan Press

Etruscan Press
Wilkes University
84 West South Street
Wilkes-Barre, PA 18766
(570) 408-4546

WILKES UNIVERSITY

www.etruscanpress.org

Published 2016 by Etruscan Press
Printed in the United States of America
Cover design by Carey Schwartzburt
Interior design and typesetting by Susan Leonard
The text of this book is set in Hoefler Text.

First Edition

15 16 17 18 19 5 4 3 2 1

Library of Congress Cataloguing-in-Publication Data

Pokrass, Meg.
  [Short stories. Selections]
  The dog looks happy upside down / Meg Pokrass.
    pages ; cm
  ISBN 978-0-9903221-2-2 (acid-free paper)
  I. Title.
  PS3616.O5565A6 2016
  813'.6--dc23

2015026942

Please turn to the back of this book for a list of the sustaining funders of Etruscan Press.

This book is printed on recycled, acid-free paper.

For Molly, Hannah, and Sian

"Never give up. And never, under any circumstances, face the facts."

– Ruth Gordon

Table of Contents

Like A Family 13

Rollerskating, Barking 15

Them 18

Goldswack 20

I Married This 21

If Things Move Under the Trees 24

Pounds Across America 26

California Fruit 30

The Agonizingly Beautiful Noses of Norwegians 33

In This Light 35

I Asked The Lord To Giveth Me A One Touch 38

Toxins 42

Vegan 44

Sparkly Plans 46

Snow-Life 48

Night Flower 50

211 Burial Lane 51

Needles 54

The Difference 55

Flapping 57

The Light-well 59

Hush 61

The Cooling 63

Elizabeths 66

Helium 69

Stars 71

Sit In Here   72
Top Shelf Syndrome   73
A Person Can Laugh   74
Quack   75
Don't You Want Some Sun?   76
Desert Air   79
Hemophiliac   80
The Cursing Wife   81
Giant Killer   82
Waist High   86
Maybe   88
Spicy, Dark   90
Toll-Free Kale   91
Queenie   92
Bus Vibrations   93
Universal   94
Fake Pearls   97
Hello, Lipstick   99
Foreign Accent Syndrome   103
This is Great Times   105
Cash Register Tape   107
Safari   109
Ringing   110
Plastic Pool   111
Books from Etruscan Press   117

The Dog Looks Happy Upside Down

Like A Family

The city is always moving its pinkie to tell me it's alive. One day it smells like steaming artichokes—another day, Lapsang Souchong tea. My friends, other secretaries, gather on the sunny bench like a bouquet. From a block away it looks as if they are complaining, bending backwards and yawning. He never liked them, or even wanted to know them, but now that he's not around, they're what I have.

I live on Carl Street near the park in a room big enough for myself and maybe a ferret, a half block from the express train. I work downtown in an office complex where I keep schedules for three generations of architects. For Christmas they gave me a robot dog and a gift certificate to Travel Smith.

My stomach twists like an earthworm after the rain. I tell myself I won't wait for the phone to ring anymore, but have waited all Saturday morning again. When it rings, I count to three, touch "talk."

"Yo Yo Ma," I say.

Calling me is probably on his "to do" list, which I imagine includes trying on new running shoes in preparation for his next marathon, meeting his training coach in her live/work space, upgrading his phone or his GPS running gizmo, catching up with his ex-wife over Dragonwell tea. Taking the kids for the weekend so she can play.

"What's new?" he asks.

He's lighting up—I can tell because his breathing sounds ragged and doggy. Rain starts drumming on my roof. I look at the ceiling, which seems to be sagging in on itself. It's not my ceiling, so let it crumble.

"I miss you at lunch," I say.

"The world is your oyster," he says. He said the same words when I told him my period was late, very late, and that we had a pink color from it all. Still, he said he was moving to London to help raise his elementary school kids. The main thing, he told me, was that his brother would never fire me—that I was like family. As long as I remained with the firm. His voice was thick, as though he'd just received Novocain.

"So we're a firmly?" I'd said, blood warming up my face like a space heater that really worked.

He didn't laugh. He never laughs.

On the phone there are silences and delays—words that could have been taken from flash cards. My voice echoes back at me, and I hate the sound of it. I imagine the glow of his cigarette illuminating London. I hang up and it all comes out. After I clean my mouth and face, I take a walk.

Rollerskating, Barking

On Saturday, my best friend, Lila, invites me to spend the night. I'm trying not to fall asleep on the couch watching The Late Late Show, which unfortunately turns out to be some gray and predictable western, when she finally lets me know the whole story. She'd been walking home alone from school on Thursday, as usual, right along Via Esperanza where we often walk together, when she hears a horn, turns, and this hot guy is staring at her, asking her where is Las Palmas Drive? She points the other way, but he just keeps on smiling a dirty, happy smile.

He probably smiled because, although Lila is only thirteen-and-a-half, she's got lips as blubbery as Angelina Jolie's. She's around five-four, and always wears platform shoes. Her hair is the color of dirty lemons, thick and long, slightly wavy. Her eyes are piggy, but nobody seems to care. They are green, like certain marbles that are hard to part with.

"Jesus, so what happens then?" I ask, lighting a cigarette from her mother's pack, fallen onto the smelly carpet. The whole living room reeks of cat pee and the smell of smoke helps block it out. Lately, I've been getting used to Merit Ultra Lights, Lila's mother brand. I like the way they make my breath taste. Just this year I've decided that I don't like smelling clean.

"Well," Lila continues, with a thirty-second pause for dramatic effect. "Then he says he'd give me a ride home." This she reports like a celebrity. Her lips seem swollen with victory. She has more to tell, and it's waking me up, begging me to pull the rest out.

"So what's his name?" I ask. Whatever it is, I'm going to hate it. "Perfecto," she giggles. She obviously doesn't remember. All she remembers is that he just turned sixteen and he's given her part of his birthday present. She runs to get her suede purse, which I love, from her bedroom.

As she flies down the hall, her hair bounces off her butt rhythmically. She's graceful. There's something about the way she doesn't make much noise when she runs, or skates, or even when she cries. In fact, I've only seen her cry once, and that was when her little brother fell off an eight-foot wall and she thought he was dead. She knew she would be blamed. But it turned out he was just knocked unconscious.

She's back from the bedroom and is holding something out to me in a toilet paper wad. She opens it carefully, tweezers a tiny hand-rolled joint. Lila and I squeal. I think it makes her horny when we smoke, because we end up running around the front yard, barking at the neighborhood dogs, her idea. We try to get them to bark back, and it works. One of them is my golden retriever, barking madly from my backyard down the block. I can tell it's him by his hoarse, pitiful bark. Occasionally, he'll actually howl, and that sounds great, like it is finally coming from the right part of his body.

We race around the kitchen, ready-made brownie mix open. Her mother is at her boyfriend's house, so there's no problem. As usual, we eat half of it raw. By the time we're in bed and ready to settle down, I have heartburn. I can't help thinking about the boy, Peter Doyle. White blond hair, a surfer's grin. I imagine them lying together, digging down inside each other like sand crabs. Lila's breath becomes regular, and I turn away from her. Sometimes I love her and hate her so much, I can't wait for tomorrow.

Them

You would hate it if you knew how many times I apply lipstick now that you're gone. I'm putting it on, like, every five minutes to get through the next fifteen, though I know they use fish scales to make it, and it's like killing fish to put on lipstick for no reason. Nobody usually sees my champagne-grape stained lips except myself and two adorable medical professionals.

If I had been a cat you probably would have kept me forever, even with an incurable disease. I think about that every time I clean the litter pan, especially late at night. I clean it too often because it makes the cats love each other more, and also because I can smell how sad I really am in the unpleasant odor of their piss, which I've read glows under black light.

In bed, my eyelids behave like cheap polyester drapes, unable to keep out the light. I wake from dreams about us walking nowhere ... covered with butterflies. I can taste you with my feet the way butterflies taste leaves and flowers. Without you here, I notice too much about how the town is changing, new money moving in, teenage girls with their rubbery, flat stomachs. They walk around cold-eyed, like billboards about nothing.

Sometimes, I drive to the Taste It where they use organic bags. As I shop, I try not to gawk at girls' stomachs like I used to try not to stare at perfect front lawns. If I had a flat stomach, and a perfect lawn, and if I were not dying—you might have stayed here on my sofa, drinking beer and burping to mark your territory.

I'm a sloth, it's what we had in common. And the fact that our left eyes feel much more connected to the intuitive parts of our brains than our right eyes do!

Also, the first time we made love, I remember how we talked about the fact that bulls are really color blind, and how a red garment has nothing to do with their rightful anger. How just having to cope with a cape being waved at you by some short murderer dressed up like a kid on Halloween would be bad enough.

The young doctor took my pulse this morning, prescribed yoga. He had stubble on his shin, and Teva sandals—like you. This guy, this doctor, made me blush when he said he liked my cockroach tattoo. He walked out to get the nurse, held her hand and brought her in to see it. She had a cute haircut, neon blue eye shadow. I told them why cockroaches fascinate me, that they can live for weeks with their heads cut off. They looked at each other, seemed to connect without touching—as if this were all about them.

Goldswack

He sent her a touch-and-talk parrot, named Goldswack. They still hadn't met in person, though he said he loved her soul, and she said she loved his.

The face of the parrot looked like the face of sex, all beaky and ecstatic and involved with its own satisfaction. She placed it high on top her dresser, above everything else.

With the captain in mind, she lay down topless and bottomless, thinking about tobacco, pipes, and parrots. Blocking out elliptical machines, hormone patches, and Skinny Cow popsicles. The pattering of new rain put her to sleep for a midday nap, and while nothing wonderful slid up or down any particular crevice of her body—when she awoke she felt as though she'd been somewhere exotic.

I Married This

My husband Gordon looked as though he'd found religion—as though he'd never tasted real food before this beef stew meal at Angie and Bruce's. He appeared to be sucking his teeth after every bite, taking his time, thinking about what he'd sucked—then stabbing a new forkful.

"I have to have this recipe," I said, giggling and poking his calf with the tip of my shoe under the table.

"Jesus, the way the vegetables blend into the meat and the meat blends into the sauce...wow."

Angela's new husband Bruce looked tired and bored. I didn't know him enough to be funny—to be myself.

Their cat, Tuna, was batting the glass door, yowling and laser-beaming her eyes on all of us.

"Spoiled fuckhead cat," Bruce said.

"Right, right," Angela said, staring at her nails, which were down to nubs. "Well as I told you, geniuses like me make things up."

Her breasts were so newly round and high, she must have had implants. I found my eyes struggling to avoid them—puzzling at how oddly they matched her worn face.

"You made this recipe up?" Gordon said. He leaned forward—his foot tapping thing starting. I could feel the vibration.

"I mean, to be able to create something like this is a gift," I said, trying not to gawk at Tuna batting the glass. The cat had always been fat, we used to joke about his waddle. Tuna was skinny now—stringy.

Bruce cleared his throat. He hooked his arm around Angie's shoulders.

"I married this," he said, kissing her cheek, his lips making the sound of suction you hear opening a sealed jar. She seemed frozen, looking at Tuna through the door.

After marrying Bruce, her son, Frank, was sent to a therapeutic boarding school ("wilderness camp"). She remodeled the bathroom—installed hand-painted Israeli tile in the shower.

～

After dinner, Angie and I hand dried all the bowls so they wouldn't chip. She was slow and thorough, her eyelids heavy. She took each bowl in her arms, tenderly blotting.

"Daria," she said, looking at me in that new way, "I did something very wrong."

She motioned me into the bathroom. Closed and locked the door behind her. I was impressed with the beauty of the tiles and the new shower design. Four people could fit.

"Secret?" she whispered.

"Please," I said, grabbing her hand hard.

"I sent him a shoe box with Pez in it. Hundreds. No dispenser, because he won't need that. Candy isn't allowed, you know. Like sending a knife in a cake." Her hand was cold, and I wished I could warm it.

"People have to do something," I said, "For you, this was the right thing."

Her chin quivered. "But to feel like a criminal for sending him a treat..."

I could hear the men clearing their throats in the dining room.

"Listen to them out there," I said. Her pupils were a shade off from purple. Hugging her, I smoothed her cashmere sweater shoulders. Her implants pressed into my ribs.

"You're a great mom," I said. I unlocked the door and straightened my shirt.

She fixed her face in the mirror, squirted drops in her eyes. Then she smiled at me, or at least, her mouth moved up.

We walked back to the dining room and over to the door, holding hands. She opened it wide. "Tuna! Tuuuuuna!" I put my arm around her shoulder to steady her.

The walls were very close. We waited to hear a rustling nearby, but all I heard were the tight voices of our men, talking quietly about the raccoon problem in the neighborhood.

If Things Move Under the Trees

The elf was alive. I was drunk, but he was alive, and he was not dry at all. Rain-wet and not very cute, a lawn elf, a.k.a. my boyfriend Kyle in a lawn elf suit…looking like a petulant child. Boy elf, kind of pretty.

My daughter had left the party. She had seen enough, with her new boyfriend sober and Mormon-looking, with large, arrogant teeth.

My Kyle was, again, drunk and wet from the rain, with the viewpoint of an imbecile. But is it normal, when drunk, to close your eyes and sing with your belly sticking out? I ignored him and went under the trees with Charles who claimed to have a motion detector. Charles said, "Let's go see if things move under the trees," and I said, "Hand me a cup," and he did. I drank what was in the cup, adding red to the four glasses of white and the two of rum with eggnog and that to the earlier death of five Mexican Wedding Cookies and one large square of homemade fudge.

"I am going to throw up," I said, looking around for a towel.

"No you aren't," Charles said picking me up, calling me a handmaiden, and ignoring Kyle-elf. Charles-the-mighty...he carried me to the trees while Kyle watched, wet with real elf tears that were incredible magic windows to his fucking elf-soul.

"You are walking backwards Charlie unicorn," I said and he said, "Because your Kyle is one helluva lawn elf again," and I said, "Does that mean we will fuckaroni?"

"Shhhh!"

Charles hissed, so I kissed his solid lips, which tasted chocolaty and strangely had the shape of my favorite coffee mug, the brown glazed one I spent some money on. Kyle knew I was no angel, but I was a hardheaded woman like in the song, and I kept things neat as a pin. Also, I liked men the way I liked the special kind of holiday M&M's...guilty and pretty.

Mainly I wanted to die in the forest with a unicorn, not in a hospital bed or on a medical chair, as all of the old people in my family had, between the last twenty Christmases. So I thought this was a step in the right direction.

Pounds Across America

On Tuesday afternoon I line up with other petite bru-
nette actresses, silently, our eyes framed with dark liner.
When it's my turn to walk on stage, the assistant casting
director asks me to smile, inspects my teeth for flaws. She
has purple hair, a nose ring, and a T-shirt that says "2nd
Butch Bitch." She looks me over—back to front to back.
Says they'll call if I make the cut.

I work in the fringes of midtown Manhattan on
the night shift, which allows me days to audition. My
co-workers are mainly out-of-work actors. Our job is
calling people who've ordered our diet product from a
TV infomercial.

The floor manager creates a sales contest to motivate
us, calls it "POUNDS ACROSS AMERICA!" We're all
nervous, fluttering and bullying each other. I pile Three
Musketeers bars next to my coffee. A bite, then a sip, then
a call. I wave at Jeremy who's been on the night shift the
last month.

The prize is Broadway show tickets for two. I dial,
opening my Three Musketeers. "Yep?" a tired female voice
says. "Hi. Is this Janet?" "Depends," she says.

"This is Martha Tiffany with Dr. Feldman's weight loss system! Congratulations, Janet! We've shipped your trial order, and you should be receiving it any time!"

"Jingle-jangle-Jesus!" says Janet D. Higgins, 190 pounds, in Racine.

"Janet, Dr. Feldman is having us call every customer individually so we can design your unique program. How many pounds do you need to lose?"

I can't help reaching for my Three Musketeers bar. I hear the pop of a fart from the young recruit behind me.

"Fifty," she says, followed by a puff of air. "Great. How fast would you like to do that, Janet?" I ask, tonguing the caramel nougat. "Three weeks? Heh!" "Let's see, I'm just looking at the chart," I say. I turn to see what's happening. Dawn (who started when I did) is doing her shtick for a group in the back, saying "Pee-niss" in a Mickey Mouse voice. "Pee-niss, pee-niss, pee-niss!" Janet screams, "Mommy needs a little time out too honey."

"Janet, we're looking at . . . (here the script suggests to improvise) . . . two to three to four months if you follow the easy step system!"

I look over at Jeremy, his new haircut. He just did a national soda commercial—knows he's hot. He's rolling a joint under his desk, not really caring if he gets caught.

"I got to try something," Janet says. I hear a child yelling.

"Let me get to the other reason I called . . . and this has to do with what we just talked about. We care about your success as much as you do, Janet, and we don't want you to have a gap in your continuation—an important concept in weight loss. We're real backed up here, Janet! People are waiting for months to receive orders because of the success they're achieving."

The script says WAIT NOW FOR REACTION.

"Oh," she says. "I guess that's good then. Was your name Martha Tif-ney?"

"Martha Tiffany Reynolds," I say.

I wave at Jeremy near the window grid, flipping me off like he always does. I stick out my tongue, and he gives me his rat face. We spent last weekend in bed, and he's probably bored already.

Janet tells me in a hushed tone that I sound like a super, no B.S. gal. "You do too, sweetheart—we love you here," I say.

She says she's a waitress. Her husband died on the way home from work one-and-a-half years ago, crushed by a semi. She has a toddler named Trevor. He's a handful and needs a good preschool. She hopes to be able to afford one soon.

Sweat is forming under my breasts and pits even though the air conditioning is blasting. I say the last line of the script a bit early, feeling my full bladder, pressing it with my hand to make it worse. "You. Deserve. Success."

She gives me her credit card number, saying "Shit yes!" to the Supreme Success Package (the most expensive).

"I bet you're pretty and thin, Martha Tifney!" she says before she hangs up.

⌒

After work I bring Janet's order sheet home under my shirt. I read off each name as I tear the sheets into bits: Kelly, Nita, Jen, Marla, Iris, Nancy, and Janet. They will be mystified when there's no charge on their statements and they receive nothing else.

I take off my clothes and stand naked in front of the bathroom mirror. Look at myself from different angles. The way a casting director would.

California Fruit

We were transplanted Pennsylvanians who understood the value of fresh fruit. The rental house had lemons, oranges, tangelos, loquats, figs. My mother let me take the bedroom that faced the orchard.

I saw him the second week. It was the middle of summer. He lay on a striped beach towel between our two yards, near the loquat tree. I went outside to say hello. I was not exactly shy, though my voice sounded it. An elaborate coconut scent surrounded him. He smiled and asked me to join him. He was tanning, though his body was already brown.

I went inside for my SPF 50 Coppertone, grabbed a beach towel, and went out to where he lay. I asked what his ancestry was, admiring his black tilted eyes and dark, thick skin.

Sioux, he said. He was one-quarter Native-American, one-quarter Spanish, one-quarter French, and one-quarter Norwegian. No surprise that he'd been exotically grafted.

He told me not to put on the sunscreen, offered me his wonderful smelling basking oil instead. He said I was pretty but would fit in better with a really good tan.

I burn quickly from the sun, and mother had warned me not to try. My dad never told me to be careful about anything, but he was dead now. I knew that Mom's voice had gotten too strong.

He told me not to worry about sunburns, assured me that my freckled skin would adapt, just like his. He asked me if I would be interested in meeting him again that night when our parents were asleep.

Climb out a window and you'll make no sound, he whispered, as if there were spies in the loquat tree.

That night I put on my nightgown and went to bed. My skin was stinging and bright red. When I touched it, it turned white for a second, then bright red again. I took two aspirin. I couldn't wait to see him again, under a softer light. I was not too young to understand what this meant.

Under the night sky, he looked as dark as a hazelnut. His eyes were thirsty. We started laughing about nothing, rolling on the ground and grabbing the grass—flicking it at each other.

It's warm tonight, he said, unbuttoning my shirt. He ran his hands over my breasts, my stomach.

"What's here?" he whispered. He put his finger inside my bellybutton, and scooped out a small fruit seed. He laughed.

"I went crazy eating tangerines today," I said. I was glad it was dark because my face felt hot. It seemed I could not get enough citrus flesh. "Juice," he said, moving his fingers inside my jeans and into a place I couldn't believe.

The next night we met again. When we took off our clothes, he stroked my irritated skin curiously, as if offering first aid.

"Soon you'll get tan, then brown, then perfect," he said.

"What is it with the tan thing?" I asked. I really wanted to know.

He flinched and stiffened. My skin got cold.

"Bugs," he said, swiping at the air. I realized my family's bad fortune could slip over me like a dark curtain.

We lay silent for a while listening to the sounds of night. I decided to tell him about a friend of mine...a girl I knew, whose father insisted their family move to Alaska. He worked for the telephone company because that was where the money was.

"She's never even had a boyfriend," I said. "Or fresh fruit," he added, bringing my hands to the place above his thighs. We did things new to me that I'd never forget.

A week later, he disappeared. I found out that he'd been visiting his aunt next door. He lived somewhere in Wisconsin. I had been so sure he was a Californian...that meeting his strange expectations meant belonging.

It was our first winter in California—just Mom and I. No cousins, no aunt and uncle, no grandparents to visit. I sent them postcards of my beautiful new land. Pictures of palm trees lined up like chorus girls. Huge waves and white beaches. Bikinied women the color of the dark pine furniture we left back home.

My chronic sunburn peeled in tiny pieces like snow.

The Agonizingly Beautiful Noses of Norwegians

Tonight, Albert Albertson took me to a foreign film at the Cinemaclub—a Norwegian film in which 10 gorgeous people died. The women had agonizingly beautiful noses. Their deaths were as agonizing as their noses, and it seemed fitting, or at least it fit, and I didn't feel as sad as I would have felt watching normally attractive people die.

The father of one stunning dead Swedish girl had a perfect nose, white-blond hair—a movie hunk, and I mean this guy was like walking sex feeling, the women in the theater needed to suck popcorn when he walked on screen, his ultra-kind glasses, and square everything and brewed coffee-colored eyes, a chin that matched his car. He probably smelled like male-musk. "Hurry," I thought. "Die if you are going to!"

My own father was round and wobbly, and had a very ugly car, and died in a quick and explosive heart attack and really that is the way I think it is only fair to go. My date, Albert, had a round nose, three-quarter moon shaped ears, but maybe they just looked so because of his unusual lack of facial structure, i.e. cheekbones.

The attractive thing about him was his wit, the funniest and only straight guy in my acting class, even his cleavage-shaped belt buckle made me laugh, and the fish on a ladder tattoo on his back, a back I had massaged before the movie, in the middle of which he turned around and started kissing my neck and I said, "I have a neck injury, be careful, and also we're going to miss the movie."

We hailed a cab in the wind, and I felt for a moment that I had betrayed Albert Albertson and was determined to charm him back. I would not reject him again post-movie, I didn't want to reject, this was my New Year's resolution.

In the movie, when Albert grabbed my hand, his warm sticky and buttery fingers circled mine, and he landed my hand on his thigh. I felt anything but wild, a tiny bit betrayed, and for a second I felt I might fall—which made no sense as I was sitting.

Albert had bad breath, and my birthday was coming. I could be a grandmother in some cultures, primitive cultures, and my tits would fall and wobble like egg noodles.

In This Light

John does not own a wall mirror. "Sorry," he says, "we can use each other's eyes to know we are human, okay?" He does not believe in reflections.

There are drops of semen on my lips when he says he loves me for the first time, and tears. I do not dry them.

⌇

Twelve hours after my husband David and his bike were destroyed by a truck, people distributed hospital smiles. My cheeks smiled back, bile gathering inside my throat.

Congratulations, you are now a bird with no tree.

They'd thought he was dead, then changed their opinions and had something to say to me when they found me sitting against a wall in the waiting area hallway. He was alive. But not his spine.

"You may have heard it wrong the first time," the hopeless/happy face of the doctor/nurse said. Someone held my hand, my hands.

⌇

David had been home with 24 hour care for just over one year when I started walking alone in the city in the middle of the night. For some reason I felt an urge to buy milk, which we were never really out of. I was not frightened under any circumstance.

One of the many nights, walking alone in Midtown at 2 a.m., I was held up at gunpoint. A group of youths, jeans swimming around their knees, blocked me, squealing, "Who the fuck said that?" They took my money, and one of them poked my nipple. I felt as though I were watching it happen a short, safe block away.

John owned the Ice Mart where I bought the milk. Every night he was there, listening to music on his iPod, talking to the few slumping, tired customers. He always stopped talking when I came in, said, "Hello, nightingale." The night I was held up, John looked at me very hard . . . but didn't ask what had happened. He offered me Kahlua, and I cried a little. We sipped from the same small bottle—watched each other's lips.

Maybe my cell phone knew something beforehand, because it vibrated often and for no apparent reason.

Now, John vibrates, I vibrate. I crave his lips, his eyebrows, the smell right below his stomach. What it makes my body feel, so stupid, so young.

~

David molds delicate cats and birds with colored clay. He can use his fingers very well now.

"His fingers do the walking!" the day nurse says. This nurse, Jill, a handsome and strong girl, has full breasts. David's eyes rest on the window.

Behind his wheelchair, on the wall—a photo of us newly married. Goofy, grinning. Redwood trees. I am wearing the felt hat with a pink cloth rose. David always said it made me look like a movie actress.

"Okay, well, I'm off to finish up some stuff at the office and grab some supplies," I say. "David, you take care of this fine girl." Jill is used to this line, nods.

"Sure thing, and David will be very happy to see you tonight," she always says.

I kiss him on the head before I leave. He says, "Aaaah, aaaaah."

His lower body is covered with a thin blanket, and this way, I do not have to see.

I Asked The Lord To Giveth Me A One Touch

When I stepped barefoot on the bee I was allergic to bees. The Jesus-man steadied me with an even gaze. My attraction to the Jesus-man may have had something to do with feeling like a fraud, which I'd been feeling for too long. Also, he had Jesus hair and a Jesus face and was the most athletic of the bunch. That is, he probably had ADHD. And my name was "Mary," which had never pleased me, I had changed it to "Maritime," but boy-howdy I reverted back to "Mary" when I met the Jesus-man.

Soon, my husband was scheduled to take his daily long run, to cover geography with trail running shoes. When he ran, I'd flee the heat and sit like a slug in the REC room at the nice, nearby lodge with Internet.

"These pretty women own pet rats," Jesus-man said, pointing to both myself and my friend Bonnie, who had joined me there and who still loved me a lot sometimes. We did have pet rats but not with us at that time. Bonnie was comfortable in a bikini, showing off in a pool or lake, and I probably would have been better in a crowded bar. We had different strengths, but our Jesus-man seemed better than us at all times. In many cases I was sure of it. He loved to be loved.

The iron was hot, I told my husband, who nodded and sauntered off to our cabin to grab a beer from the cooler. We had listened to the sound of a neurotic bird in the tree next to us for too long, he and I.

"You have not yet found a grass snake?" Jesus-man asked.

"No, but I asked the Lord to giveth me a OneTouch," I said.

Just then: Sunburned, butt-slapping apostles came out from the lake for salty corn chips and margaritas and to razz the women who were mostly reading magazines, and one of the followers, the father of the worst-nosed girl and a Buddhist who chanted in the open, outdoor theater, said, "What's wrong with Mary?"

Jesus-man said nothing, his long hair dripping while he popped a can of coke.

I said: "Well, you know, grass snakes urinate on touch." And I almost said, "Which sounds better than most things."

That would not have impressed him. I was not funny enough to impress him. My jokes sucked, and thank God I did not have a son who would love me too much despite it all.

I liked to be in a group away from the women, listening to the non-chatter of men about steak and whiskey, with cute men walking in front of me and the one walking behind me and my husband carrying our books.

"You are going to order the waffle?" I asked my husband who had silently returned.

"Yes," my husband said and went back to reading.

The bee sting foot was puffing up and purple and white—and a crowd of friends, not true friends, but friends who were friends of friends, were oohing and pointing at it. Plus, I was wheezing. One "friend" ran off to the camp office to get a doctor.

Did Jesus-man seek sex in the dark? If so, I bet he was, it was...was good. The night before our last he offered me some bug spray when we were walking to the outdoor talent contest. He handed me a rag and said, "It will work even in the swamp." And he sang for me.

I said, "You say these bugs are everywhere, and boy are you accurate."

"Comes with the territory," he said. Then he coughed and spat and smiled and made the sign of peace.

I tried not to look at my belly pushing out of my shirt.

"Oh, girl," he said. So we were laughing, but I thought about the sin of enjoyment and how it led me through tall grasses, like a human train. I wanted to be in his gallery of humans. He was a great guy, a trip-master, looking for a green snake to talk about. This may have had something to do with a desire to meet up in a hotel somewhere far away.

That night at home I imagined how we may have been like teenagers inside a VW van, old Jesus-man and I, and I have a little more pride now and don't do that anymore...but then again mostly my pride is charred. In my fantasy, I pulled jeans from the hamper and he threw on a glass shirt. I asked him if I could brush his hair. In the fantasy he said, "Yes," and for hours I did that, kissing it and brushing it and braiding it and handling it as if it were my own.

Toxins

Irina cut our hair when we lived on the hill. She was a blonde Russian woman who wore pale powder, fake eyelashes, and blue liner. She rented the tiny beauty shop on Polk—two chairs near the window, turned away from the sun.

One cut she told me about her ex—how he left her with no money. Their teenage son was taller than her now, and stayed with his girlfriend too often.

Men all want one thing, she said. Even my own damn kid. That time she styled my hair round like a mushroom.

My husband Leif and I were still newlyweds who stacked tofu boxes and refrigerated safflower oil. We lived next to a Chinese beef jerky factory. Toxins floated in our window. All the newspaper stories were about cancer. Skin cancer, throat cancer, pancreatic cancer. We didn't have enough money for furniture, much less cancer.

Leif became irritable the day of his trim. He swore while he was shaving in the morning, cutting himself more than usual.

"What's the matter?" I asked. "She flirts with me," he said. "What a bitch," I said.

I imagined him a small child on the beach at Long Island Sound, his mother leaving him alone for a sec while she put on her suit. Something about Leif was unnaturally vulnerable. He had serious asthma most of his life, and lived with too much worry.

We went together. When she saw me, her face reddened. I picked up a *Vogue* and sat quietly while she cut his hair.

"You two are like a comedy team," she said.

As if to illustrate her point, Leif told her a joke about how much hair he was losing because of my tofu lasagna, my Tempe casserole, the lack of meat in our diet as if I were poisoning him. I felt my hands get cold—though I tried to fake a chuckle.

Irina laughed so hard she snorted, doubling over as though she were losing urine. She cut his hair deeply, winking at me grotesquely. When we walked out Leif was nearly bald on one side.

A week later, walking to the health food store we noticed her windows were taped. A sign in the door said "FOR RENT." The shop was dark.

We saw it as somehow our fault, purchased expensive algae tablets from the health food store to fight off cancer. We swallowed bits of ocean each morning before opening the windows.

Vegan

Beth had glitter makeup that someone gave her. I wondered who. It was still sealed, she'd never opened it, and it was in a small box of unused makeup—stacked with other belongings. I knew she would want me to have it now, so I brushed it over my cheeks and eyelids. It made me look alive, and I smiled at my face in the mirror. It was still my face—a face that was born looking spoiled.

"Don't ever talk to me about boys or meat," Beth said on her last birthday.

"You mean men?" I asked.

Beth forgot we were grown up a lot. Nothing mattered as much as the fact that she couldn't find any size twos, and I was trying to help on the Internet. When we were little, her hair smelled like teriyaki chicken. I remember telling her as though it were the highest compliment. She pulled my arm so hard I never wanted chicken again.

"How would you like to be fried?" she had said.

She was a vegetarian, a vegan, and eventually bones and skin.

The doctor said it was not because of her diet; it was her brain making her body die, and then it finally did its job. One stupid nurse said that to my mother, about her brain being in charge. Mom turned to the chair Dad would have sat in, and said, "See?"

Sparkly Plans

A few months after chemotherapy, Mom got a part-time telemarketing job selling ballet season tickets. She didn't sell enough, though, so they fired her after just three weeks.

Mom said she hated selling people tickets they didn't want. She would tell people not to buy anything over the phone if they sounded old. She was proud of getting fired.

Unemployed, she still sends money to Friends of the Homeless and Save the Trees. I worry about where she is finding money to do this. I look at old photos of Mom from when she was an actress—her hair all modelish and her eyes full of sparkly plans.

These days she wears hats and wigs. But nothing makes her look normal. The new baby-chick fuzz on Mom's scalp feels so soft that sometimes I pet it and say "nice fuzz," but Mom touches her scalp too much. When she does that, even at the beach art show, even where everyone is supposed to be interesting and artsy—she looks like a bald woman fingering her head.

"I'm sick of it all, and I could use some emotional sup-port!" Mom says. She talks about how I was born with colic, wanting nothing to do with her milk. I've learned to let words fly past me.

Mom is on a very restrictive diet prescribed by a nutri-tionist. Our kitchen overflows with unbleached sesame seeds and tofu duck.

I make a mental list of our recently unlucky things: We adopted a dog who looks sad but was supposed to make us feel happy. Dad died making an old building new. The front of our house is sinking into the ground.

To protect my future luck, I've become good at: Brightening my nights by moving balled-up socks around the softest part of my body. Touching the doorknob three times before leaving home. Chopping onions with my eyes squeezed shut.

Snow-Life

I'm reading my five-year-old daughter Eliza a story about a boy and his dying grandfather. The boy talks to the moon about sadness. Eliza has her jaw set like my mother's, the day she went into Hospice.

"Dumb, dumb, dumb, dumb!" Eliza says. "Where did you get that book?"

"People die. So do animals," I say. Her bed is messed and warm. She still holds her blanket like it's part of her body, moves it around as skin.

Eliza is starting Sunday school. Ryan died when she was one year old, and she doesn't want to know about her own father, which makes little sense to me.

~

I hear the whoosh of plumbing next door and raised voices, a family argument.

It sounds nice.

"Daddy is part of nature now, and it's very, very cool, Eliza. He's part of the flowers and the mountains, like the book I read explained."

Eliza pops explosive lip-sounds.

At dinner she announces that she wants to touch snow. Right now. The kind you see on television.

"Why do we have to live so far away?" she screams. She throws herself down on the rug and cries.

~

We live in a slow, small town in Northern California. Our neighbors wouldn't do anything to help if we fell over dead, but I like it pretty well here. Everything still feels new.

Around the holidays people take their kids to see the interactive snow exhibit at a mall in the city. The exhibit is called "Winterness." This is where I have taken Eliza for a few years, but this time, she doesn't want to go. Often, I wonder how Ryan would have dealt with Eliza. There is no handbook for this child.

Near Christmas, Eliza shows me her new concoction: frozen dish soap and water mixed together in a Tupperware. She calls it Snow-life.

She rips bits of half a roll of toilet paper, climbs the piano and releases the bits, jumping around.

"You were wrong mommy! It's here again!"

She looks at me with eyes like stones under water, so angry and wet I don't know what else to do but stare.

Night Flower

You don't go to the party because you want to flower alone at night, and the color of your face is a shade off from young, and the trunk of your car is so easy to break into that you don't want to park anywhere.

You head back to your springy apartment missing the frustrating charm of night bugs, and because people would watch you enter the party naked in your clothing because this happened again, you wanted a man's body too much.

And you would not like the exit. You would not like to say, "Bye, I'm leavin' a bit early here, so damn tired!" and nobody looking terribly sad.

AND you go home early because his laugh makes you feel him in your cheap shower, soapy and relaxed...just what you would do with that if he were there too, but you can't.

You go home early because he won't do anything with what is staring him in the face. I mean, there is something not at all useful about it being there at the party.

211 Burial Lane

Gray cycles by and stops at the front yard where Jim and I live...at 211 Burial Lane. He and Nance live at 467. Their kid Carly is our Sophie's age and best friend, both of them now in middle school.

Since preschool, our kids were inseparable, Jim and I would cover our ears as they imploded in a tangle of squeals and arms and legs and long, long hair in our living room. They'd run after the other in the front yards as if being chased by the devil, then hang on the other like vines. They kept this up all these years, sleepovers every weekend, and Carly feels like family.

Now, Carly has a boyfriend, and the girls fight. No more horsing around.

Perched on the little ridge of chipped bricks, I tell Gray about the new rat in our garage. He tells me about Carly's boyfriend and how weird it feels to see his daughter all head-over-heels. Also, he saw a thing on Animal Planet about rats and how intelligent and affectionate they are. He says I would have loved it.

Nance trapped and killed a baby rat recently in their garage, he said. She was proud of herself, but it made him sick.

Our garage has rat issues too. Rat intelligence is propaganda, according to Nance and to Jim, our rodent-phobic spouses, so Gray and I end up discussing this stuff in hushed tones as if we are guilty of worse.

"Romans didn't distinguish rats from mice and they were called Rattus Major or Rattus Minor," he says, giggling.

I giggle too, because it is so crazy, and would like a pet rat and to name it Rattus Major. This may be something I will do when I am old and people can't get mad at me.

Nance is knitting the world's most amazing blanket for the new baby; she has shown it to everybody. I know what a resourceful, practical, knitting, baking, gardening (and rat-killing) woman Nance is.

Gray and Nance are no longer separated, as they had been for a few months last year. When Nance conceived at forty-two, I tried to come up with lots of funny stories about unexpected pregnancy.

I feel my face warming even with fog and summer chill because Gray is standing close smiling down, with his cinnamon cologne or whatever he wears, so I run to get something out of my car, yelling "The lint-roller is in the CAR, I need to find it. I have cat hair all over my life!"

"Ha ha, the lint roller in the CAR?" Gray says.

"Anyway, who cares!"

I am digging into the back of my car for the lint roller. I want him to ride away now and go back to his wife and the blanket she is making, and to give up on rats. Then another part of me says, Stay.

Jim, for about four years, has played computer games until 4 am and sleeps in the den, not our bedroom.

It is as if Gray knows and is trying to pull it out of me, suggesting little walks sometimes. I can always find a reason to stay at home and get things done, because I do not trust myself on a walk with that scent and his love of rats and his face. Under piles of crap in the backseat of the car, I find the roller, and to demonstrate that I am not making it up, I hold the lint-roller up high above my head, as though I am the Statue of Liberty.

Needles

Forgiveness is everything, the acupuncturist tells me. He says I have toxic rage—that's why I get so many bladder infections. Jabs eighteen needles in my arms and legs.

At the hospital, my hand is warm enough to touch mom's cheek without her flinching. The doctors and nurses don't know I dance at The Sauce, smile at me with respect. Not mom. That's why she's dying. If she could talk, it wouldn't be better.

Before I leave, I tell her the story she told me when I was a kid, about the old castle everybody forgot about because it was so dilapidated. A princess lived there but nobody knew. She sang inside the curling walls, the stones that tilted.

Later, after the show, a bulbous man in a black Mercedes says he'll pay for a photo. Just you and me, he says. When he puts his arm around me, I'm still sweating from the lights. I look like a Martian in the gold tassels and pointy hat without the other girls dancing near me. I can tell he cuts his own bangs.

The Difference

Dad never asked me and Josh what we thought, but he told us what he thought, and the little ways he could teach us about life were the most important things, he said. He took it upon himself to spend time on difficult lessons, like teaching us to drive, taking turns sitting on his lap in the driver's seat. I knew the difference between good and bad.

Dad had a screwdriver and a wrench and we named them: the screwdriver was named Bill and the wrench was named Bob.

Josh preferred Bob, because he was thick and looked sure of himself.

Sometimes Bob and Bill took walks together and talked about getting spanked so much, how they handled that feeling of oatmeal in the throat.

"This is a claw hammer, this is a needle-nose pliers," Dad said. He let us hold them.

"But this is a flathead screwdriver."

I saw what he meant, the difference was clear, so many ways to be a tool.

And I could see him reaching into his pocket for his medicine. He took it without water for his headaches and his moods.

"Which little piggy stays home?" he said, holding one or both of us in his lap until we felt like one piece.

Flapping

Bill had talcum powder on his elbows and knees, just bits of it, and he wouldn't tell me why. He said it was a short drive to Reno. There were bundles of his life kept private. I thought, better not to ask. Always this was the right decision. Not to say or do something.

My head fit snugly into his arms, and when we first met, I thought I had landed and could finally stop flapping. He seemed like a fair person. He wrote words for songs and played a little bit on his guitar.

His guitar was named "Hopper." He loved to think of himself as a hippy, called himself "Dennis Hopper." I didn't know who Dennis Hopper was, but he sounded hard to pin down.

~

An hour from Reno, I felt sick. My stomach bunched up, and to scare back any vomit, I put my head down between my knees.

He looked at me instead of the road. "I have to pee. I can feel it."

He coughed into his hands and rubbed them on his jeans.

The day felt too long. Driving with Bill took a person's hours and changed them into problems.

"You need to stretch your ass anyway," I said.

"It's bad for your disk."

Having to vomit had something to do with it, but it wasn't the whole reason.

He swerved the car, and took us onto the shoulder of the highway. He told me to get the fuck out. I did, I got the fuck out of his car.

He told me I was rude to him. He said, "You have no respect."

He said my mother was the same way, and he was not willing to live with my mother inside of me. Truly, my mother was a bossy person, and our baby would have these genes and I thought about it at night.

I'd spent my life trying to make up for Mom's bossiness. For example, I would always apologize to waitresses for ordering water with ice. Then I would thank them more than once. All of my thanking made people nervous.

The shoulder of the road felt cozy, better in a way than the car. I imagined how many people had ended things this way, stepping out of a car.

"Should I get back in, Bill?" I asked. He wasn't looking at me; he was looking out the back windshield, clucking his tongue.

Outside, it was windy. My hair flew around. Cars buzzed past like mosquitoes over water. The highway smelled like meat.

The Light-well

The rain comes in spasms, outside where nothing ever sleeps in the city it is wet and cold and crappy, the long waits between eye twitches on Zoe's face, and then the moment in which she lays down and actually, finally falls asleep.

It is winter and the doctor in the ER let Zoe go home, and there is sadly no tent over our pigeons in the light-well which is (we admit) pigeon suicide. All rustle, coo, and bird eyes circling for hawks, the occasional flap of them. And every few months, a new nest will get flooded by rain.

Our apartment where we hide from the trot of the city is an imperfect box which we like with all of its flaws and pigeon problems. We rent movies or else have arguments about whose turn it is to cook, splurge on ribs most Fridays after work.

Since Zoe was mugged and her shoulder broken, her hair feels like straw—and when she talks she occasionally trembles. I do the shopping and splurge on whole wheat crackers and goat milk, the only kind she can drink, and promise her stuff like, "Soon I will buy a big pot and make you noodles and rice until you are all good again." I really plan to turn the little kitchen into a kitchen.

Her mouth hurts, and she's riddled with stress-induced canker sores and bloodshot eyes, not pretty (for once). Among other things, her parents do not know about the mugging, and mother will castigate her for being in the subway.

She asks me to call her mother and tell her about the mugging, leaving out the worst. I feel bad for not having volunteered earlier. "Of course."

"You are not a peripheral friend," she says.

I laugh, and say, "That makes it sound like I **am** one."

She nuzzles my neck, and I decide there is nothing more thrilling than calling the conservative parents of my lover, people who voted for Jesus in the last election and wear red, white and blue hats and slippers—people who will end the wonderful times we are having here.

As I dial the phone, we both watch a new torrent of rain suffocating the light-well.

Hush

It was the second day of the Palm Springs vacation with my sister Helen and her boyfriend Ron. Helen had already taken ownership of the air-conditioned bedroom, complaining of cramps. I was fifteen years younger than Helen, who was nearing thirty. Her bedroom door was locked, and I could hear the AC blasting.

Ron and I watched *Animal Planet*. He sat on the couch, I sat on the floor. I fanned myself with my sun hat. We laughed at the faces of parrots—the way they looked so confused.

Snack food and juice in the refrigerator. I thought of carrying out napkins, chips and salsa—serving him. I didn't know how to be around men, not having a father or brother. They were usually in need of something, and I would never know what. As a child, I might be running around, pouncing. That would be fun—attacking Ron.

That first night when they fought, and I heard Helen call him a bastard, and Ron call her a psycho—I slept on the couch where it was fairly calm. Still, I only slept two hours.

Mainly, I sat in the living room, drawing my feet. I loved them. They were small, size six.

"I sleep with a snake," I heard Helen say in her low voice. Maybe I misheard.

At home, I slept with the cat.

I thought Ron looked tired, and Helen was taking diet pills again. I imagined her dead—what mother would say and if we would somehow die also.

I wanted to sleep next to him. She hated him, anyway. The idea went straight into my stomach and pinched. I reached for his beer bottle to sip from. He made a sound of disapproval when I wrapped my lips around it. Said, "uh oh."

I wanted him to see my new breasts, really nothing else. He would say if they were nice. If they were okay.

"Ready to swim!" I said. This was true. There were tiny beads of sweat on my neck and brow.

"Hey, your sis is probably asleep. That pool sounds good."

"Yeah, out then," I said.

I was going swimming, a normal impulse, and Ron could follow. Free country. I had my bikini under my clothes, threw the dress off over my head. He grabbed his towel, and through the door, I could feel his eyes on the parts of my skin which were sunburned and peeling.

"Hush little baby," I said to myself.

Outside, the pool was shimmering, and the world, with Ron trailing behind me—felt overcooked.

The Cooling

Todd, her brother's best friend, has been her only buddy for weeks now...and he persuades Kim to join him watching the newlyweds in the house on the corner. On weekends, the newly-marrieds fuck late mornings. A yellowish meek curtain frames their bedroom window like an invitation. Days have been so boring, humid and long, and looking around for stuff to do—they've run out. Paul has been away at technical camp, gone six weeks, and will fly home tomorrow.

The newlywed woman looks to be about a hundred pounds of extra weight or else pregnant, with cellulite on her thighs and butt...and the man has long hair. Plump women like to wear black. Todd and she spy from the crook of the plum tree. Kim has come to enjoy spying, but sometimes says, "Yawn."

This one though, the one they see today, is memorable. The wife gives the husband oral sex, kneeling on the floor as though by a drinking fountain. Todd catches on to what is happening first, says "Shh!" even though Kim isn't talking...his mouth rounding into a nest.

Watching it makes Kim squeamish, so she watches Todd's mouth and her face gets hot. To quiet her pulse, she thinks about her brother's face, her brother's return. They watch until the end. Then they slide off the tree.

Todd and she have simply run out of things to do. They've played board games and computer games and skateboarded at night.

Today is the day—they'd printed and signed a contract to dash across the train tracks thirty seconds before the train the Sunday before Paul came home. They both like the idea of spicing things up and pissing off Paul when he finds out. Overall humidity is nearing one hundred percent, and Kim says, "We should be wearing goggles and flippers it is so wet."

Todd's hair is longer than hers and probably makes his neck hot. He looks like a girl, tall and angular with model straight gold hair and see-through skin. His eyes are the blue of pool lights. People think Todd and her brother are fags, and they are used to it. They even laugh.

Kim knows she is pretty because the boys at school do not talk to her. Todd does, and for this reason, until her brother gets back from music camp, Todd is hers.

She imagines Todd will notice her electric magnetism when she drinks from the Boone's Farm Strawberry Hill bottle. Todd brought a beat up and rusty corkscrew, and she brought the wine from her brother's closet...only she coughs when Todd is concentrating on twisting the corkscrew in just right, and the explosive sound, a cough like her mother's, messes things up.

Some cork penetrates the bottle.

"Fuck," he says, and shoves the bottle into his mouth first, gulping loudly, and spits cork like tiny fish.

"What time is it?" he asks. He has a stopwatch, but not a real watch like Kim. She doesn't answer and takes the bottle into her mouth, wrapping her lips and slugging it. It tastes like Robitussin. He's not looking at her, trying to dig something from his pocket. She feels as though she's going to throw up, and counts silently with her eyes closed.

Todd rarely smiles. She feels sorry for him because of his massive overbite, which has never been corrected. She tries to imagine what Paul will say about the two of them watching sex and then getting a bit drunk and running in front of the train... only she's losing track of why she'd tell. Todd farts and laughs, then makes a "phhht" sound with his tongue and teeth. Kim swallows a few sharp cork bits. Maybe she's never felt so adult.

"Hurry," he says.

They walk briskly to the tracks. It is almost time, almost. He moves in close to her and touches her shoulder, and she is not her brother. He kisses her on the lips quick and dry. As in the movies, she looks up into his face. He promises to run in front of the train right after her, five seconds later, counting loudly.

Elizabeths

I tell Henry that I've always been called by my formal name, Elizabeth, but I like to invent unusual spellings: *Elyzabyth, llizabethe, Alisabethre.*

Henry calls me 'Elizabeths.'

Though we are sleeping together every night, sharing one comb, snuggling like animals, he warns me that I am not his type. He is a professional dancer, so it may mean that I am not exotic or graceful enough.

What is your type? I ask. He flips through the New Yorker and lands on a cologne ad featuring a gorgeous man lying on a marble floor.

~

At work on Monday, I charm my six architects into giving me light work only. I say I have my period. Recently they've discovered that I make many errors and they protect me from the manager. When they pass my desk on the way to coffee, they look like they're trying not to giggle, that they know I'm some kind of con artist in this job.

The newer architect, Sammy, invites me to dinner. At a North Beach pasta place, I try to be interested. I ask, "How old is your mother?"

~

I discover an elaborate vegetarian entrée online and it is beautiful and I chop vegetables for an hour, building an igloo of carrot, yam, zucchini, yellow and red bell pepper, and thick asparagus. When Henry arrives from his dance rehearsal, sweaty and hungry, he helps arrange the pieces. He's wearing my favorite T-shirt, the one that says, "I used to be a plastic bottle."

Enticing him with a gin and tonic before dinner makes it easy to seduce him. He weighs less than I do, so skinny, and is drunk after a few sips. By the time we eat the igloo, he is melting.

~

When did you first fall in love? I ask.

"When I was ten," he says, "I fell for an outfielder."

"When I was ten I fell in love with Ms. Wheelright, my fifth grade teacher!" I say. "A woman!" It was true, nobody loved her the way I did.

In the morning, Henry says, "Elizabeths, I can't see you anymore." I cry, plead. I offer him a place to live rent free for good. Home cooked food.

He sits down again. His stomach growls and he looks suspiciously like old photos of my father.

~

Sammy comes in with wrapped up yellow daisies for me. They look cheap but it is very kind. He has a large freckled face and it is reddish.

The last important contract I typed for him read "greed" instead of "agreed." He didn't tell anyone, just quietly showed me. He probably knows I'll get fired soon and the daisies are pre-funereal.

~

I soak in hot sitz baths. Henry doesn't call for two weeks. I use Dead Sea salts, lavender and herbs, flower remedies, and I say "I have a good life" to myself. I look at my naked body in the mirror, pink from the bath and it is lush and I say "What an idiot."

I pull at my split ends while trying Henry's number again. I write him an e-mail and it says: I have a problem with this. I detest this. I don't deserve this. But I don't send it. Instead, I whittle off pieces of my fingernails, and pull the skin off my upper lip.

~

The day I'm fired, I notice the architects whispering, hunched like buzzards. The Human Resources Director tells me this: Instead of current fees I typed current fleas. Instead of stick with it I had typed sick with it.

Sammy asks me out for dinner because he says he will really miss me. When he smiles, his freckles widen.

Helium

Carbonated Cat is my favorite drink. It's my sixteenth birthday. This was what Mom and Dad always concocted for my birthdays, this kid-cocktail. Mom mixes spicy ginger ale with Grenadine but adds plenty of Tequila to her boyfriend Daniel's.

We sit out on the porch and watch the leaves curl under. Mom says we should all toast to me.

Daniel says there is nothing to toast to. Mom is very still.

Daniel says, "Let's toast to the great idea that this young lady may become something some day."

There are sharp, coughing noises from a motorcycle down the block, and farther, down the block, the old guy screaming to his dog a million times as though the dog were possessed.

I throw my glass and it crashes into the weeds. Mom and I are standing, and I tell her in a loud voice what he is—what he did in his car. It is not embarrassing anymore.

He says I am full of hateful lies and what a spoiled little tale-spinner I have become.

Mom is taller than I have ever seen her.

"Get the fuck out of here NOW! And get some help! LEAVE!"

Daniel's face is red and he looks like a fat, old man. He can't do much about it since I am calling the police and he knows the neighbors are listening.

He goes inside to pack up, and we sit there holding hands, Mom and I, tightly knotted like helium balloons trying to stay here on earth.

Stars

Dad whispered, "Let's look at all these stars!"

He taught us to love French bread and goat cheese, he taught me the language of the night sky. The sad truth, the way he said it, was that a person couldn't compare this to anything else.

The second night, our hiking guide asked me if I knew how much he wanted to share a tent with me. Flicking feet, warm toes inside a creek, taking a break from hot sun and endless walking, I could figure that out.

My sister had a great mug collection, each colorful mug for each colorless Christmas without Mom. Dad trilled the hard 'r' sound when he said "stars." He slept outside the tent in his sleeping bag and purred up at them. Life moves forward, and the air inside a tent becomes liquidy.

I touched my hiking guide, Mike. I told him I never want to ever be called 'Baby.'

Losing the life of a spouse or a mother can turn a person into someone who can't decide. A person who says, "From now on, I want to be told what to do."

There will only be one man who lingers on the word star . . . stroking them with his mind while saying it.

Sit In Here

A little drunk, we share a cigarette. So cold and clear, stars pop like bugs in the sky, and my right ear hurts with a crashing pain.

The sledding hill looks lumpy and it bothers me. He tosses his coat on the snow as though it were a beach towel, plunks down, says for me to sit.

"You," he says, "Sit in here."

He opens his legs, and I sit up against him like a wall while he warms my ear with those piano fingers curling over. I let my mind do things, and then I stop it from happening but it happens.

He lives in dreams with me but he wants it to stay that way; a scene in a movie right before the middle when the popcorn is still perfect. I'll follow him into a deep blue anything.

Top Shelf Syndrome

When vertigo sets in, I mentally search for the librarian, the red haired, very new one with a delectably delicate yet shrewish face. She's tall enough to rescue me from my life-long top shelf syndrome. That is, a syndrome in which I fantasize about what is up there. Librarians grow like oxalis around the crust of the town. There is no such thing as a diminutive librarian down our way, and the dreams I have at night about this one involve ladders and falling and being caught. Me falling, her catching me and cannibalizing lips with lips, the brush of a pencil between us, her saying, "Jesus Christ," and myself answering "Hi ho!" and she saying "Bang the drum slowly," and me saying "I'm allergic to chemicals." As usual the dream ends too soon, and I wake to the toxic-lemon smell of cleaning fluids upstairs, an adult smell, which has something to do with the reason I never left home.

A Person Can Laugh

In a cafe, we ate potato salad and drank Italian sodas. I laughed at his stupid jokes, because they really were funny.

All around us, sad people walked happy dogs. A dachshund cannot ever really look like shit.

I let him rub his hand on top of my knee. I didn't even blink, just sat there like an empty driveway. He was in charge, and I had one hundred dollars left. My car needed everything.

"Do you want anything else?" he asked, and I did not. The potato salad sat heavy in my stomach. Hunger seemed like the tiniest part of being alone.

When we had sex I thought about Laffy Taffy, the way it destroyed a person's teeth, how kids couldn't care less. I would never wish to be that young again. Once things are ruined, a person can laugh.

Quack

He tells her this: "When ejaculating, I quack."

"Promise?"

She's poking water next to him—tipping front, then back, and then over again, looking at the sky, sideways.

He gets her feathers moving in such a good way. Shy, yet it does not impair her ability to look directly back, into his bright, bright bill.

She looks away, then straight at his bulbing eyes.

He amuses her with whispers of his friend's attempt to corkscrew females with promises of Fritos.

"Fritos," she tells him, "never work with me."

She bubbles, preening her drab brown sweater— terrible next to his bright bill.

As he climbs her, she paddles and slaps water as though she can go somewhere.

Quack!

A middle-aged woman, strolling the pedestrian path with her husband, says, "How come, in duck-land, the male is so goddamn beautiful?"

Her husband, slight of hair, not quite her height, puts his arm around her.

Don't You Want Some Sun?

When I asked Mike why he was always walking around the house naked, he told me he had too much to hide. That was the year his mother sat on the train tracks, and the same year his brother fell in love with small two-seater planes. The kind that break when they hit birds.

Also, Mike had lost his job and refused to send out resumes. He said there was only so much anyone could do, he was sick of worrying, and when someone wanted him—they would holler.

I'd gotten so used to Mike's nudity that I'd stopped noticing his penis crouched like a worried squirrel. I'd started feeling nauseous about meat and could no longer eat chicken. There was something about all of his skin, all at once—blending with the smell of olive oil on salad. Also, the scent of dope made it hard to notice anything good or warm about the house anymore. Always, there was a drawn shade.

"Don't you want some sun?" I'd ask.

"No, goof," he'd say. "I want some privacy, can't you tell?"

"Sure," I'd say.

Once, I said, "I'll bet if you wore clothes sometimes, you would be able to have really good privacy."

A day later, he left. When I got back from the vegetable market, his note said, "Jim and I are testing his plane and I'll be gone a few weeks. Take care."

One of our dogs was blind, but very affectionate. She slept in the bed with me, right where Mike had. Moon was nicer than Mike had become, and she had silky hair. She'd gaze into my eyes and steal my resolve to keep things clean, hairless. I held her, imagining Mike and Jim skimming over the edges or else the tips of buildings, trying not to die. Laughing, and almost letting themselves crash. Looking into each other's bursting, purple eyes.

~

I was not the kind of person who liked to go out—but now, all I wanted was to be free of the house. I drove from coffee house to coffee house. I tried out every customer bathroom.

And I found myself staring at Jerome, who made perfect espresso drinks. Young women lined up, thrusting their tits out. Jerome had full lips and well-shaped chin-stubble. Dark curls, like a Caravaggio painting.

He seemed to make a great deal of eye contact with me. I wondered if this was my imagination. Curious, I would stand in line waiting for my latte, shy.

"Latte for Jean Veevee!" he called out. I did not correct him when he mispronounced my name.

And then, one day, I did.

"Genevieve," I said.

"Huh?"

"Genevieve?"

"Oh fuck," he said.

"No, no! It's fine. I just, well, I come in here, a lot, and I thought I should tell you."

"I am the worst," he said. "That is a rockin' name!"

I did have nice hair, and my skin was nearly unwrinkled due to a lifelong struggle with agoraphobia. When one never goes anywhere, the sun can do little damage.

～

Mike called from Nevada. My guess was Las Vegas. He said he was in a tiny town called Primm. I pictured his worried squirrel. I imagined he was finally warm.

"How is the plane doing?" I asked.

"Oh, good, really good. We are really…really doing, good."

"No plane crashes?"

"Nope, I'm in one solid piece!"

I heard a sound which grew to fill up the holes inside the phone, heated up the metal. A woman's sound. A giggle.

"Piece?" the voice said.

My breath caved in like a paper airplane—stabbing the wall, the floor.

Desert Air

Second day at the summer cottage, my bikini is damp. My hat is hiding, playing an evil game. I pour a little of mom's Kahlua in a plastic cup, lick the sides. Yesterday I kissed a root beer-skinned boy who said he'd meet me at the pool today at one o'clock.

My big sister watches, perched on the sofa, a sweater over her shoulder, staring at invisible graffiti on my body.

"See ya," I say. She gives me the finger, goes back to her book about time travel.

Outside, the desert air is a blow dryer. By the pool my boy looks me over as if I dropped from a tree, as though there were no yesterday. He seems not to remember me at all. Diving in, he slices through water.

Hemophiliac

Mom's silent smiles were the worst. She wore her "I'm a hemophiliac" pendant all the time since dad left. Mutts would scoot back a bit, enough to get out of her way.

"Muttsy!" I hissed, when mom was working. "Stop licking your dick."

I wondered how much he knew. How much can dogs know? He sat at the window every afternoon, waiting for Dad.

"Her blood doesn't clot," I said.

The tip of my nose itched but I refused to scratch it. The ground was unstable because so little had been done around the house. Spiders bubbled up through the floorboards and Mutts chased them. We were both afraid of the big ones.

Some things were better. I liked the flow of the house. The slippery way light bounced off the new yellow walls.

The Cursing Wife

He made his new wife promise to curse over the phone as soon as he got to the hotel. He'd take his shoes off and call her. This took the edge off. It felt delicious and naughty. Boy, could she lay it on!

Her unquestionably creative words were better than a Manhattan or a White Russian.

Holding the phone tight to his right ear, smashing his fleshy earlobe, the way she put together combination specialties, over and over, and how much he wanted her, as though illegal. He imagined her spittle flinging itself against the phone. Her small boned face and delicate, wet teeth. Juicy words just bursting out.

Giant Killer

We meet at a Divorced Devout's potluck. He is as cute as Jesus would have been after playing racquetball. Sweaty and ropey, smiling like a choir boy. This week I joined the group. A big step.

I sit on the same side of the picnic table as him, that first day. He has Jesus-blond hair, short and bird-fluffy.

How many men have I kissed right here in this very spot over the last forty years? One. Morris, who left me for an atheist waitress at Hooters. Now I am a middle-aged sinner.

He says his name is "Goliath." An adorable lie.

I fidget a bit, beat my foot to an old John Denver song, "Sunshine on my shoulders makes me happy..." and continuously look around behind me as if we are being stalked by Lucifer.

An enormous sadness radiates from him. I want to gather him, break his bread and let it melt in my mouth. I want to make him forget his ex. I am wearing heels and stockings, a short yellow dress, which hugs my body. I adore men of a certain type—this type. He is Jesus plus Meatloaf meets The Little Prince. Shorts, white T-shirt, pot-belly peeking out...a sexy rock-star curl to his lip.

I'm a townie. A lonely woman with a great love of unique pot-holders. I already want him.

I slide my face up close beside Goliath's cheek and say what's that scent? It hardly matters what he answers—he turns his head and gives me his business card. A-Promise Insurance, Bill Bithers, four phone numbers and three e-mail addresses. His eyelids are soft and sweet. Though he sells insurance, I am undaunted.

⌐

The next night I drive to his houseboat. He's invited me for celery and dip. He no longer has the same, fluffy hair. Butch as the devil himself. Athletic, creamy generous pectorals, unexpectedly vulnerable against his sea-captain tan. He is dominant; he will always be dominant. My Goliath.

I bend down, kiss him with lipsticked-lips.

We share a bottle and a half of Chianti, sitting on the deck of his houseboat, watching the twinkling island of Alcatraz.

Later, on his captain's cot, he moves against me like gently lapping water. I kiss his chin and taste celery dip. I slither my hand over his rock-candy-mountain. He playfully pushes my hand away. We are halfway-to-hell in a spinning-teacup; this is a game, we both know what is happening here. He is here...I am here...we are divorced and unholy and I am moist and perky as a peasant. He can have his way with me, because he is a giant-killer. Now! I rasp.

"I won't break the good china!" he squeaks. Nothing makes sense, which is fine.

Soft sleek digging hard moaning wide with want; my singing mouth is next to his deaf ear.

It's VERY OKAY!

Is this nice? Do you like this? Is this what you like?

Divorce has done its damage. I beg him to thrust his giant-killing club into my Dragon's Lair. He nods, kneels on the bed and skips into me with his staff, holds me like that for so long I can't wait for the songbook. I grab feverishly for his invisible hair with my hands.

He pushes and I am gasping full arched bodiless mindless somewhere else entirely. He rides the Christmas of me with his bishop. I am his prisoner; he has been here before. He has always been here and will always be here, keeping me on this exquisite edge; when I finally give it up, it is with a sob of relief, prayer and sorrow.

We lie in a tangle of non-alcoholic punch and limbs. His eyes are closed and he is far away in some other memory. We create a circle of energy. His skin tastes like rummage sales and Christmas bake-offs . . .

⌒

In the middle of the night, we wake to the sound of a foghorn or a text tone. Before I can stop myself, I am on top; he is under me and I am holding him close; Mr. Knish is instantly happier in my velvet donation box, which elevates my belief tenfold. When I sing Hallelujah he says to bring it down a bit, there are dogs in the neighboring houseboats.

I am ready again . . . or ready still . . .

We breathe together in some half dream of divorced pleasure. I am in his arms...it is late...

Giant killer! I know he will break my heart. The ending is already written into the beginning. Nobody can make us married again in the next half hour.

~

I drive home before dawn, catch the end of *The Trouble With Angels* on AMC. Before falling asleep, I give the cats a few treats. They have never seemed more ravenous.

Waist High

Their neighbor came over with a bag of lemons, camped in the hall and watched her make tea in the kitchen. She was wearing slippers, and Sam was out for an eighteen hour run, training for an 80-mile race. He said the lemons were waist high and quite "fierce." It was always about lemons for anyone who lived on the block. Sour fruit intimidated people.

Really, it wasn't a good idea, wouldn't fly, to keep bringing her lemons when she was alone. And she hoped it would never stop. But she didn't know what to do with them.

What do you want me to do with these?

"Make juice, I guess. Or pie?" he said, looking at an old photograph on the wall of her daughter, two-years-old, at the beach.

Well, be more exact. What do you want me to do?

I like it when a woman knows what to do. This is what she imagined him saying. She wished he would say this. And she wished that she were the kind of woman who would squeeze a lemon for him with her lips and have him watch. She knew he wanted this.

And she wanted him to drink the lemonade, not whiskey, the way some men did, even after very long runs. To hold her hand, and to tell her that her husband would be okay. To kiss her while telling her that she would be okay, too. And then, to whisper "Will I be okay too?" So that she could make something with so much fruit.

Maybe

I notice the short guy in places that make no sense, churches, tracks, banging his backpack against his hip. I see him near the bookstore, a place to stay dry from the rain. Later, I will say to him that he has a MAYBE stuck to his face. He will say that his face doesn't know what it is saying.

There is nobody home. He touches my hair, as if he is here, I say, "Hey, there is nobody else here," to the dog. But I smell him. Somebody is really touching my hair.

I am smoking again. It is getting worse. Women here discuss dog food ingredients and how many calories it takes to eat a carrot versus how many calories are in the carrot itself. They talk about which actors they think are hot and which actresses they think are sluts. They haven't said more than "hey" to me, it seems. I may not be here at all, which is comforting. Their earrings are so heavy they don't know how to smile.

I live alone but I have the dog who looks sad when he's right-side up. Best to try and get him to roll. I wake up to sun and weeds, a canopy of TV talk, the loud neighbor's SUV and once again no milk, no eggs.

Anyway, the short guy may be married. Or else, this could be his day, he may crave a beer and ask me to accompany him and I will do so. That's what townies think a woman like me would do, and I'd hate to disappoint them.

My husband Ezra used the word "frigid." That word died in the last century, I told him. Ezra died in this century. Now my body is the opposite of frigid, it is horribly alive.

The short guy asks me if I drive a car. He can't, he's too short. Bad idea, he says. For sure, I say. No driving and drinking.

We have a few beers at my house, then whiskey. We do what living people do. Afterwards, he falls asleep on the dog's chair.

Laying on his back, gazing at the ceiling with wet eyes, the dog looks so happy upside down.

Spicy, Dark

She had gone to the store for butter and gin, and when the door closed we were finally alone. Your mother had a way of hollering at us for what lived criminally in our brains because our brains were fresh and new.

The minute the door closed, you kissed me, using the tip of your tongue scientifically.

Then we sampled your uncle's beer, the stuff he brewed. He called it "Froggy, Dark".

~

I was all about trying, I said later, on the rug.

You peeled back up straight and looked me in my face to make sure it was okay, and that I understood what I was doing. I was younger than you by a year, unused to a boy's body unfolding.

"It's nice," I said.

"Okay, let me show you how," you said.

"This here..."

"Okay."

My head on your stomach, I liked what was happening, all of it; the feeling, the scent, the way things bloomed up so ripe and quick, just for me.

Toll-Free Kale

During the day, my husband snores in rhythm with the dog. Some may say it is cute. I would not say that exactly. Today, two or three beautiful women on Facebook offer me favors. One offers me something I'm too embarrassed to speak about, and another offers virtual grapes. Ken offers to leave Facebook and does. There is something wrong with my home phone—my land-line. It rings, and the caller ID says "Toll free kale." I knew Ken was gay from day one. It is difficult for women like myself to accept certain things about the world's Kens because they are perfect for us. Another vague come-on from a Facebook friend goes like this: "I am a very straight man, but a lesbian in my soul..." I'm sure some men are, inside their souls, lesbians. Yet, if I wanted a woman, I would find a woman. Also, I am married. My husband is sleeping right next to my computer. The dog and he.

Queenie

Queenie was fucked up . . . said she didn't have a motor left, and that was sad? Did we know?

I said, "Yeah, scratch your name in the sidewalk and where's that asshole with the Adam's Apple and the dog?"

"Bran?" she said.

He calls himself "Bran?" I laughed.

"Fuck Bran," I said, by then she was asleep.

Little girl legs and zits like galaxies, bitter crinkled eyes, half-moons.

Her boyfriend had sliced her pinkie off was the thing. Bran.

I asked her forever, does it hurt?

"Nope!" she said in such a happy voice it made me think she was not going to wake up. She was safe now with the rest of us in the park.

"Kin, kite, hole," she said, touching my hair with her soft, remaining fingertips.

Bus Vibrations

The vibrations of the California bus wake me from another dream, the kind of dream that makes me hop on my better foot until it sweats. The bus is gassy and sounds as though it's saying 'oops'.

People get off the bus looking sorry and mad and clumsy, interrupting each other's bodies, robbing each other of something.

I can't shoot my words straight anymore . . . it's as though someone has turned my electricity off. Since he disappeared, there is nobody to hear me.

Everyone knows how a man's eyes dart like bullets toward soft new hills. Young men wear rain-repellent clothing and do not use umbrellas. In movies they own iguanas and parrots and have affairs with funny women.

But today, what matters is that I own a new cell phone—and that my cell phone, when it rings, sounds like a cat fight, or like a different woman.

Universal

Mom didn't want me to bring her, but I didn't give a fuck. If the dog were all slobber and destruction, I wouldn't. Star was a lap dog with feathery fur, with eyes like a cartoon dog's, round and sad.

"You brought it!"

"Yeah, well, shit, Mom, I couldn't find a dog sitter. Do you know what they cost? And, you know, she'll be shy and sleepy. Sorry, but nothing to fear," I said.

My fleece shirt was punctuated with dog hair. I'd forgotten my lint roller. Mom's vibrant womanish tunic showcased violet flecks or else grains of silk. It was holiday-cheery in an environmentally happy way.

Star sniffed my mother's Birkenstocks, tongued mom's toes. Mom whimpered like a congested child. "It doesn't like me," she sniffed.

"Foot licking is a universal dog greeting," I said. "Star!"

Star stopped—wide-eyed, so goddamned pretty, but stunned, as though a bone had just been thrown into an invisible force field. She moved anxiously. Mom had an odd effect on animals.

Star aimed her focus and took a flying leap for my arms. I was standing, unsupported, and the force knocked me over. Star had such a feminine yet muscular body.

The impact to the back of my head was what I imagined being shot at very close range felt like. I grabbed at my coat to catch the blood. The back of my head had landed on one sharp, decorative squiggle at the base of mom's faux antique umbrella stand.

I often wondered who would die first and in what kind of horrible way—myself, or my former boyfriend, Richard, who was too tall to be living modestly in China.

Mom said, "Honey? That was quite an impressive whoopsie." "Mm?" I moved my lips, while trying to hide the bleeding with my raincoat, which was both absorbent and reversible.

"Where did you say you got your dog friend?"

Mom had never owned Band-Aids or bandages or any kind of first aid tools. When I was little, I had to mop cuts with my clothing or ask neighbors for Band-Aids. Mom was phobic of blood.

"Star belongs to Richard," I said.

I was crying a bit but from the pain and about Richard being dead.

Richard left me for a ribbon-thin bitch from Hong Kong. It would have been impossible to ship the dog to him, to them.

Mom said, "God works in such fascinating ways."

I sat up and saw real stars on the floor. Star licked my chin. I could taste metal in my mouth. I kissed Star's nose to let her know I wasn't mad, as she already seemed repentant, her tail between her legs, licking her right paw, nursing it.

"Oh, sweet girl," Mom said, her face pruning and unpruning. Half her face in a shadow. Today she was so nice. I was sure I could bring myself to hug her.

I ambled toward her with sleepy-bear arms extended, willing to let her warmth and closeness comfort me, the smell of martinis hanging like a halo over her head next to the ripe smell of heavily nurtured flowers.

"Would you like to see my Bluetooth phone?" she said, backing away. Mom turned away from me and screamed with her hands over her eyes. I hoped it wasn't the dog.

I could imagine the final street she'd walk away on. The street would be called Rosemary Lane, and would be narrow enough for a line of Mini Coopers, a pretty street devoid of cars.

Fake Pearls

It's Thanksgiving, and I wake up thinking about Nana in the kitchen, 30 years ago—basting an enormous bird. I loved dark meat, and she'd smile as if that meant something wonderful about me.

She left me three framed sketches of an organ grinder monkey—hearing no evil (hands over his ears), speaking no evil (hands over his mouth), seeing no evil (hands covering his eyes).

I remember the quiet way she stood up from the table one year during the half-fed moments before dessert— my cousins making jokes about Nixon's nose, wiping their chins. How the backyard was completely dark that night. Her light blue dress harmless as a wild rabbit between the hedge to the neighbor's and grandfather's voice like a balloon rising over the table, the way he'd clap his hands, "You kids should get your own TV show and make some money."

Sometimes I can't help myself around the holidays, call to hear my ex-husband's voice.

He'll laugh. "Bake me a rhubarb pie and cover it with vanilla ice cream, you know what I like." If his girlfriend answers with her mouse brown voice, I hang up.

This morning I hear the neighbor's vacuum and the Macy's parade on TV. Their kid is off at college, one died in a car accident.

Here, where the air is white and thick in the city near the ocean, we hide from each other behind double-paned glass—but we know the basics.

Thanksgiving dinner is at my nephew's tonight, his wife is a vegetarian. Their new baby will be dressed up in organic baby clothing—crying or smiling. At dinner, there will be Ginseng Cola, tofu turkey and stuffing. I'll wear fake pearls.

Hello, Lipstick

A new family moved into the house at the crest of our cul-de-sac. Dad said he could tell they were Russian. My brother Liam and I put on *Back in the USSR* by The Beatles and danced in the living room.

Dad said "Hello lipstick!" as the Russian mother, wearing an orange-red scarf around her lanky hair, went right to it...mowing the front lawn. Slippers, shorts and a man's long T-shirt, her eyes appeared as if they stung or had stingers in them. She looked a bit trashy or hung-over. I knew men liked this kind of thing.

"How do you know they are Russian?" Liam asked Dad.

"Russian women are all about hard physical work and pearly lipstick," Dad said. Liam smirked.

Ma had been gone for a week to help Tessa set up in her new apartment and life. Tessa was 22 and had moved to Hollywood to pursue acting, was studying in a prestigious acting school in Pasadena. Dad's right eye jumped around, but he was still handsome. When he started visiting a psychiatrist a year ago or so, he weighed 190 pounds. Now he bragged about being 180.

His moods were more even, but he seemed tired and fell asleep about four times a day.

Using Dad's toenail clippers on my nails, it occurred to me that mental problems (like freckles and moles) might be contagious.

My sister, Tessa, would never touch anything he used.

~

The Russian kids looked down at their feet a lot and seemed to drift in and out of their house. They had flat faces—pale and exotic.

The girl, a year or so younger than me, did not wear lipstick. I was starting to wear lipstick. The boy did not come out often, but once I saw him walking briskly around the cul-de-sac.

Dad was off of salt, which is why I hoarded little salt packets from the burger place for Liam and me when Ma left. I made sure there was at least a bit of salt on everything we ate, even ice cream.

"Is there a father?" Liam asked.

"Dunno," Dad said. "Maybe he's fat and in hiding."

Maybe, I thought.

Liam was mostly silent when Dad spoke to us. When Dad passed a lint roller over his shoes, Liam looked the other way. I pretended not to look at anything.

That night, Dad had a challenge for us. He asked us to dress up as a kind of Russian animal or human...and pretend we were brand new in this country.

Ma had a friend checking in on us, and in just about an hour, Eileen would be over with an egg or cheese. If we were in costume, Dad said he would turn out the lights, close the drapes, and let us move around in our costumes with privacy. He said we could use any of Ma's clothes, but not her hats.

"Warning—in order to win this game you both have to act very Russian in your own way, be original and not unreal!" Dad said.

I didn't want to worry him about what I did or didn't believe, so when I walked past him I moved carefully. I knew Dad did not want Eileen to visit or even knock on the door. I'd put on Ma's lipstick and made a snow hat out of hiking socks. I tried to make myself a James Bond beauty. Liam's costume was Ma's belt. I had no idea in what way her belt made him look Russian. Liam shrugged and said, "Subtle-like."

I told Dad and Liam my name was *Octavia Galore*. Dad dusted off the DVD player and put in *From Russia With Love*.

"You look glamorous!" Dad said.

"She looks like a homeless freak," Liam said.

"This fucking movie is great and we do not have to even watch it to feel that!" Dad said. He gave us our scores. My score was in the millions. Liam's was in the hundreds because Liam hadn't really tried. The phone rang about every hour.

At midnight, bedtime...Dad told us Ma would pick us up soon, in the morning. Ma was going to take us to California.

"I know this sounds weird," he said. "I'll be going away in the morning."

I hugged him hard and realized he felt thin and loose. Liam chased me around the house with a flashlight. Dad stayed in the garage, in his car, with the Rolling Stones playing in his CD player, "I'm so hot for her. I'm so hot for her. I'm so hot for her and she's so cold!"

Foreign Accent Syndrome

At the dog park, I saw her walking her mother's Yorkie. I hadn't seen her in over a year. I had always admired her eyebrows, simple even roads on her face. Her lips turned down, even when we were kids, waiting for lemons. She told me about her foreign accent, and not sleeping for three years. These things add up, leave their mark, she said, in an accent that sounded like fake British.

Everyone knew the head injury from the car accident nearly killed her. She'd been thrown—they found her nearby. There was a name for what she had. She said the neurologist explained it so well, Foreign Accent Syndrome. Most people thought she was a bitch as soon as she said hello.

Would you like to come over later and hang out? I asked. I had nothing planned.

She seemed pleased, wrote down my phone number and address.

"I'm not very modern, I'm afraid," she said.

Her fancy sounding accent whizzed overhead like a dragonfly—harmless, colorful. When she smiled, her lips changed direction, charged up her cheeks.

Later, she arrived on her brother's old moped wearing wasabi green clogs and a backpack carrying all she couldn't hold: Slippers, backgammon board, tea bags, a dainty spoon for stirring.

I never lose, I told her after the first game. She cried. I made tea with honey, she put on her slippers. I put on mine.

This is Great Times

I met him in the bar part of the restaurant, when my brother went to look for the woman of his dreams. The man sat there alone, talking to his napkin as though it were funny.

"But I also love steak and oysters!"

"This is great times!" he said.

"I'd join you, but I'm off to find the bathroom or to the middle of nowhere," I said smiling, draping my coat over the chair next to him.

⌐

"Ever made love?" I asked him, about two hours later. We'd been talking about nothing, watching the others say stuff.

"No, no, but I love watching porn," he said.

I excused myself again.

No matter what the situation, I can find my brother dancing with a fat woman, or himself.

"Well, I love to have fun," I said to my brother, who does not.

The man with the napkin was crying, when I returned. It seemed creepy and I knew I had been sarcastic, but it was part of the quest for fun.

"Hey, I'm a good listener," I said.

And it is true. I love to find out what makes a man cry.

Cash Register Tape

Her job was driving from gas station to gas station, selling specialty cash register tape with ad space on the back. She sold it to gas station owners and mini-mart managers. Ads like "FREE WASH WITH ANY FILL!" printed on the back of cash register tape, the stuff people usually threw out.

She knew how to simulate enthusiasm because she was an actress. She had been studying acting since age ten—having been to an acting conservatory, she knew how to approach a role.

Practicing her smile in the mirror, she threw the cash-register tape in loops around her own shoulders like a lasso. The trick was to position the tape around a decision-maker's shoulders, get him touching it, eager for what came next.

Back at her office she smoothed her hair. It felt both slick and hard. She was close to winning the monthly sales award, and if she won it, she planned on buying a new outfit, setting up another interview with a theatrical agent.

~

One of the owners was Sammy. He had two Beagles and a wife who was living somewhere else. Sammy had the worst breath she'd ever sampled, and it made her wonder if he were gravely ill.

He took her out to see a violent movie in an IMAX theatre, ordered an extra-large popcorn to share. Watching the movie, with his hand planted on her knee, she listened to the sound of him eating unbuttered popcorn. How each piece squeaked in his teeth. She believed she'd come to forgive this sound.

Later, driving up along Mulholland Drive, he stopped on the side of the road early in the morning and fell asleep. She didn't bother to wake him. To him, she was a cash register tape girl.

She thought about "Nina," a role she'd played in Chekhov's "The Seagull"—the world of Russia, a hundred years ago. The life of a young actress, losing her mind.

Safari

He asks me to sit, talk a bit with him on their stairs. His wife is away again, on safari.

From the sidewalk, their house is a three-layer cake with tangerine frosting. It's nice to be inside it. I sit next to him on the lovely stairs, feeling lucky.

The tip of his finger is grazing my nylons, making little circles. My nylons have a run the shape of a neck.

"Poor stockings," he says, moving his finger in smaller and smaller circles around the tear.

"Nets of hell. Be glad you are a dude and your legs are allowed to have air," I say.

"Speaking of 'dudes,' never trust one of us when we are on safari," he says.

"Oh?" I say. I can't look at his mouth.

"Because we come across these limping animals just …grazing."

Ringing

"Dolphins swim in the soul when it is calm," the king of television yoga says. His face seems so relaxed. Suddenly, you feel the heat, and must remain quiet to remember, again. Later, you will hang with the regulars at Dew Drop, and forget about it. In accordance with enlightened people, human beings are caught between Venus and Mars, may as well revel. You're sitting there watching TV when the phone rings and you will not answer this time. This is the first time you just let sound swim inside your house.

Plastic Pool

The pool was four feet deep, and we bought it at Target half off. You could float on your back and think, "fun times are here," because at least you weren't burning hot.

Mom and I watched it fill up with hose water. She looked around at the back yard, the neglected fruit trees, and said, "I've got to call those idiots and make sure they get a gardener." It stunk from rotting fruit and dog poop.

I wasn't going to worry about anything. I would just float on my back in my bikini. I would be weightless. There was an annoying fleabite in the crook of my arm, which I sucked on.

The pool was going to be my way of making more friends. I was sick of the two friends I had from last year. Lila and Blythe were both considered to be strange. Lila wasn't ugly when she washed and brushed her long hair—about once a week. She memorized animal facts. Blythe looked like Pinocchio. She was a violin prodigy. She had a European hair cut—short, black, severe. She was proud of her breasts, which were large, adult size. I didn't have any breasts yet, but the doctor said not to worry.

I wanted to know if late development meant small breasts. Mom said it didn't, that she had been the same way. "Worth the wait," she'd say with an exaggerated wink. Now that dad had his own place and his bipolar disorder, she had all kinds of new expressions.

In my new pool, I would float on my back when it was dark, looking at the stars. Nighttime swimming had been my dream.

Since there was no one else, I invited Lila and Blythe for a nighttime dip on Saturday. Lila couldn't come because her family needed to drive to Oxnard. Blythe said she sure as heck would be able to make it. She was all about night-time and pools and stargazing.

"Show me the big dipper," Blythe said. "I want to make sure you know which one it is."

Blythe was wearing her bikini bottoms, but she left her top on the side of the pool. The pool seemed much smaller with her beside me. I was glad it was cheap.

Terribly absent were Lila's cigarettes. I pointed to the area of the sky where I saw the Big Dipper. "Uh huh," she said. "A long bent ladle, right?"

Blythe looked wet and slick—her womanly breasts gleaming. I felt angry at her for taking her top off.

"It looks like a crooked dick," I said. The pool was a bee cemetery. I scooped two up and threw them out.

"I don't even really know what a ladle looks like," I added.

I could hear all the neighborhood dogs talking to each other. A bee might have been marching down my arm. Something tickled.

"You know what a crooked dick looks like?" Blythe said. Her face was large, or maybe it was the moon.

"Not exactly," I said, trying not to let my eyes get caught on her nipples, "but I've seen them, and they all have different shapes."

"So, like...whose?" Blythe asked.

"I haven't seen that many dicks, I..."

The water in the pool was getting cooler, the smell of new plastic making things worse. I hoped she hadn't peed in the pool, though I would not put it past her.

"I have a lot of cousins," I said.

She smiled at me so brightly then, she almost looked pretty. She squealed, half laugh, half death cry. She said she was getting cold—hey, what a great idea, let's bake oatmeal cookies.

Suddenly she said, "Could you imagine sucking one of those?"

"God, no," I said, fast and soft. Her eyes looked back at me big, full of thought. She moved in.

"What do you imagine they taste like?" I knew better than to speak.

"Corn on the cob," she whispered into my ear, spitting, "with a bit of salt."

This was not happy news. I knew that violin prodigies lived exotic lives, they were much older than other teenagers. They traveled to Europe.

I imagined Blythe kneeling in front of an audience, her mouth open like a baby bird. "I'm not ever going to do that," I said. It sounded fake, as if I were acting in a play.

Blythe moved to the far side of the pool. The moving water sounded smooth. She kept still, cupping her chin in her hands. I wondered if our friendship was done.

Her nose was cartoonishly off-kilter, as if a person had sculpted the middle of her face blindfolded. She practiced three hours a day after school, was going to be on CD covers wearing velvet dresses. She was going to be rich. She already knew everything that was going to happen.

Books from Etruscan Press

Zarathustra Must Die | Dorian Alexander

The Disappearance of Seth | Kazim Ali

Drift Ice | Jennifer Atkinson

Crow Man | Tom Bailey

Coronology | Claire Bateman

What We Ask of Flesh | Remica L. Bingham

The Greatest Jewish-American Lover in Hungarian History | Michael Blumenthal

No Hurry | Michael Blumenthal

Choir of the Wells | Bruce Bond

Cinder | Bruce Bond

The Other Sky | Bruce Bond and Aron Wiesenfeld

Peal | Bruce Bond

Poems and Their Making: A Conversation | Moderated by Philip Brady

Crave: Sojourn of a Hungry Soul | Laurie Jean Cannady

Toucans in the Arctic | Scott Coffel

Body of a Dancer | Renée E. D'Aoust

Scything Grace | Sean Thomas Dougherty

Surrendering Oz | Bonnie Friedman

Nahoonkara | Peter Grandbois

The Confessions of Doc Williams & Other Poems | William Heyen

The Football Corporations | William Heyen

A Poetics of Hiroshima | William Heyen

Shoah Train | William Heyen

September 11, 2001: American Writers Respond | Edited by William Heyen

American Anger: An Evidentiary | H. L. Hix

As Easy As Lying | H. L. Hix

As Much As, If Not More Than | H. L. Hix

Chromatic | H. L. Hix

First Fire, Then Birds | H. L. Hix

God Bless | H. L. Hix

I'm Here to Learn to Dream in Your Language | H. L. Hix

Incident Light | H. L. Hix

Legible Heavens | H. L. Hix

Lines of Inquiry | H. L. Hix

Shadows of Houses | H. L. Hix

Wild and Whirling Words: A Poetic Conversation | Moderated by H. L. Hix

Art Into Life | Frederick R. Karl

Free Concert: New and Selected Poems | Milton Kessler

Who's Afraid of Helen of Troy: An Essay on Love | David Lazar

Parallel Lives | Michael Lind

The Burning House | Paul Lisicky

Quick Kills | Lynn Lurie

Synergos | Roberto Manzano

The Gambler's Nephew | Jack Matthews

The Subtle Bodies | James McCorkle

An Archaeology of Yearning | Bruce Mills

Arcadia Road: A Trilogy | Thorpe Moeckel

Venison | Thorpe Moeckel

So Late, So Soon | Carol Moldaw

The Widening | Carol Moldaw

Cannot Stay: Essays on Travel | Kevin Oderman

White Vespa | Kevin Oderman

The Shyster's Daughter | Paula Priamos

Help Wanted: Female | Sara Pritchard

American Amnesiac | Diane Raptosh

Saint Joe's Passion | JD Schraffenberger

Lies Will Take You Somewhere | Sheila Schwartz

Fast Animal | Tim Seibles

American Fugue | Alexis Stamatis

The Casanova Chronicles | Myrna Stone

The White Horse: A Colombian Journey | Diane Thiel

The Arsonist's Song Has Nothing to Do With Fire | Allison Titus

The Fugitive Self | John Wheatcroft

YOU. | Joseph P. Wood

Etruscan Press is Proud of Support Received from

Wilkes University

Youngstown State University

The Ohio Arts Council

The Stephen & Jeryl Oristaglio Foundation

The Nathalie & James Andrews Foundation

The National Endowment for the Arts

The Ruth H. Beecher Foundation

The Bates-Manzano Fund

The New Mexico Community Foundation

Drs. Barbara Brothers & Gratia Murphy Fund

The Rayen Foundation

The Pella Corporation

Founded in 2001 with a generous grant from the Oristaglio Foundation, Etruscan Press is a nonprofit cooperative of poets and writers working to produce and promote books that nurture the dialogue among genres, achieve a distinctive voice, and reshape the literary and cultural histories of which we are a part.

etruscan press
www.etruscanpress.org

Etruscan Press books may be ordered from

Consortium Book Sales and Distribution
800.283.3572
www.cbsd.com

Small Press Distribution
800.869.7553
www.spdbooks.org

Etruscan Press is a 501(c)(3) nonprofit organization.
Contributions to Etruscan Press are tax deductible
as allowed under applicable law.
For more information, a prospectus,
or to order one of our titles,
contact us at books@etruscanpress.org.